PUFFIN

DIARY OF A WIMPY KID
Do-It-Yourself Book

BY JEFF KINNEY

Diary of a Wimpy Kid

Diary of a Wimpy Kid: Rodrick Rules

Diary of a Wimpy Kid: Do-It-Yourself Book

Coming soon:

Diary of a Wimpy Kid: The Last Straw

DIARY
of a Wimpy Kid
Do-It-Yourself Book

by Jeff Kinney

YOUR
PICTURE
HERE
↓

PUFFIN

PUFFIN BOOKS

Published by the Penguin Group
Penguin Books Ltd, 80 Strand, London WC2R ORL, England
Penguin Group (USA) Inc., 375 Hudson Street, New York, New York 10014, USA
Penguin Group (Canada), 90 Eglinton Avenue East, Suite 700, Toronto, Ontario, Canada M4P 2Y3
(a division of Pearson Penguin Canada Inc.)
Penguin Ireland, 25 St Stephen's Green, Dublin 2, Ireland (a division of Penguin Books Ltd)
Penguin Group (Australia), 250 Camberwell Road, Camberwell, Victoria 3124, Australia
(a division of Pearson Australia Group Pty Ltd)
Penguin Books India Pvt Ltd, 11 Community Centre, Panchsheel Park, New Delhi – 110 017, India
Penguin Group (NZ), 67 Apollo Drive, Rosedale, North Shore 0632, New Zealand
(a division of Pearson New Zealand Ltd)
Penguin Books (South Africa) (Pty) Ltd, 24 Sturdee Avenue, Rosebank,
Johannesburg 2196, South Africa

Penguin Books Ltd, Registered Offices: 80 Strand, London WC2R ORL, England

puffinbooks.com

First published in the English language in 2008
by Harry N. Abrams, Incorporated, New York
(All rights reserved in all countries by Harry N. Abrams, Inc.)
Published in Great Britain in Puffin Books 2009

2

Made and printed in England by Clays Ltd, St Ives plc

British Library Cataloguing in Publication Data
A CIP catalogue record for this book is available from the British Library

ISBN: 978-0-141-32767-9

www.greenpenguin.co.uk

THIS BOOK BELONGS TO:

_____

IF FOUND, PLEASE RETURN
TO THIS ADDRESS:

_____

_____

(NO REWARD)

What're you gonna do with this thing?

OK, this is your book now, so technically you can do whatever you want with it.

But if you write anything in this journal, make sure you hold on to it. Because one day you're gonna want to show people what you were like back when you were a kid.

WOW, HE WAS INCREDIBLY SMART AND WITTY EVEN **THEN!**

IT'S TRUE!

Whatever you do, just make sure you don't write down your "feelings" in here. Because one thing's for sure: this is NOT a diary.

Your DESERT

If you were gonna be marooned for the rest of your life, what would you want to have with you?

Video games

1.
2.
3.

Songs

1.
2.
3.

ISLAND picks

Books

1.
2.
3.

Movies

1.
2.
3.

Have you

Have you ever got a haircut that was so bad you needed to stay home from school?

YES ☐   NO ☐

Have you ever had to put suntan lotion on a grown-up?

YES ☐   NO ☐

Have you ever been bitten by an animal?

YES ☐
NO ☐

Have you ever been bitten by a person?

YES ☐
NO ☐

Have you ever tried to blow a bubble with a mouthful of raisins?

YES ☐   NO ☐

EVER...

Have you ever peed in a swimming pool?

YES ☐ NO ☐

Have you ever been kissed full on the lips by a relative who's older than seventy?

YES ☐ NO ☐

Have you ever been sent home early by one of your friends' parents?

YES ☐ NO ☐

Have you ever had to change a diaper?

A LITTLE HELP?

YES ☐ NO ☐

PERSONALITY

What's your favourite ANIMAL?

_____

Write down FOUR ADJECTIVES that describe why you like that animal:

(EXAMPLE: FRIENDLY, COOL, ETC.)

_____   _____

_____   _____

What's your favourite COLOUR?

_____

Write down FOUR ADJECTIVES that describe why you like that colour:

_____   _____

_____   _____

- -

The adjectives you wrote down for your favourite ANIMAL
describe HOW YOU THINK OF YOURSELF.
The adjectives you wrote down for your favourite COLOUR
describe HOW OTHER PEOPLE THINK OF YOU.

TEST

ANSWER THESE QUESTIONS AND THEN FLIP THE BOOK UPSIDE DOWN TO FIND OUT THINGS YOU NEVER KNEW ABOUT YOURSELF.

What's the title of the last BOOK you read?

_____

List FOUR ADJECTIVES that describe what you thought of that book:

_____   _____

_____   _____

What's the name of your favourite MOVIE?

_____

Write down FOUR ADJECTIVES that describe why you liked that movie:

_____   _____

_____   _____

- -

The adjectives you wrote down for the last BOOK you read describe HOW YOU THINK OF SCHOOL.
The adjectives you wrote down for your favourite MOVIE describe WHAT YOU'LL BE LIKE in thirty years.

Unfinished

Zoo-Wee Mama!

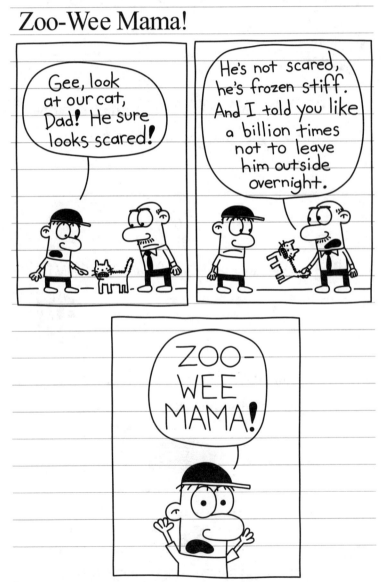

COMICS

Zoo-Wee Mama!

Make your

OWN comics

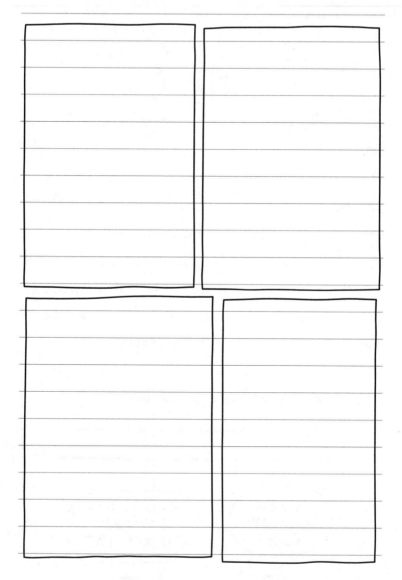

Predict the

I TOTALLY CALLED IT!

AW, RATS!

I officially predict that twenty years from now cars will run on _____ instead of petrol. A cheeseburger will cost $ ____, and a ticket to the movies will cost $ ___. Pets will have their own _____s. Underwear will be made out of _____. _____ will no longer exist. A _____ named _____ _____ will be president. There will be more _____ than people.

The annoying catchphrase will be:

_____

_____

WUBBA DUBB, MY TUBB?

RAT-A-TAT-TAT AND CHICKEN FAT!

FUTURE

Aliens will visit our planet in the year _____ and make the following announcement:

_____

_____

The number-one thing that will get on old people's nerves twenty years from now will be:

_____

Predict the

Robots and mankind will be locked in a battle for supremacy.   TRUE ☐   FALSE ☐

Parents will be banned from dancing within twenty feet of their children.   TRUE ☐   FALSE ☐

People will have instant-messaging chips implanted in their brains.   TRUE ☐   FALSE ☐

FUTURE

YOUR FIVE BOLD PREDICTIONS FOR THE FUTURE:

1.

2.

3.

4.

5.

(WRITE EVERYTHING DOWN NOW
SO YOU CAN TELL YOUR FRIENDS
"I TOLD YOU SO" LATER ON.)

Predict YOUR

What you're basically gonna do here is roll a dice over and over, crossing off items when you land on them, like this:

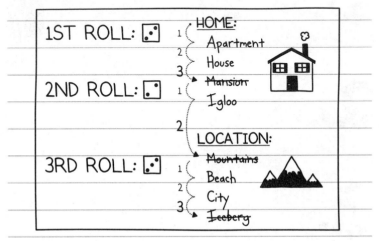

1ST ROLL: 🎲

HOME:
1. Apartment
2. House
3. ~~Mansion~~
   Igloo

2ND ROLL: 🎲

LOCATION:
1. ~~Mountains~~
2. Beach
3. City
   ~~Iceberg~~

3RD ROLL: 🎲

Keep going through the list, and when you get to the end, jump back to the beginning. When there's only one item left in a category, circle it. Once you've got an item in each category circled, you'll know your future! Good luck!

MY LIFE STINKS.

future

HOME:
Apartment
House
Mansion
Igloo

LOCATION:
Mountains
Beach
City
Iceberg

JOB:
Doctor
Actor
Clown
Mechanic
Lawyer
Pilot
Pro athlete
Dentist
Magician
Whatever you want

KIDS:
None
One
Two
Ten

VEHICLE:
Car
Motorcycle
Helicopter
Skateboard

PET:
Dog
Cat
Bird
Turtle

SALARY:
$100 a year
$100,000 a year
$1 million a year
$100 million a year

Design your

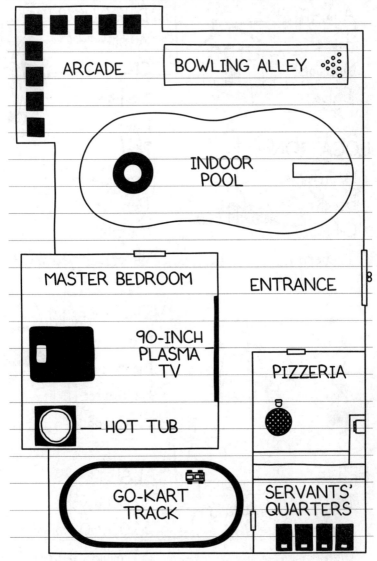

GREG HEFFLEY'S FUTURE HOUSE

ARCADE

BOWLING ALLEY

INDOOR POOL

MASTER BEDROOM

ENTRANCE

90-INCH PLASMA TV

PIZZERIA

HOT TUB

GO-KART TRACK

SERVANTS' QUARTERS

DREAM HOUSE

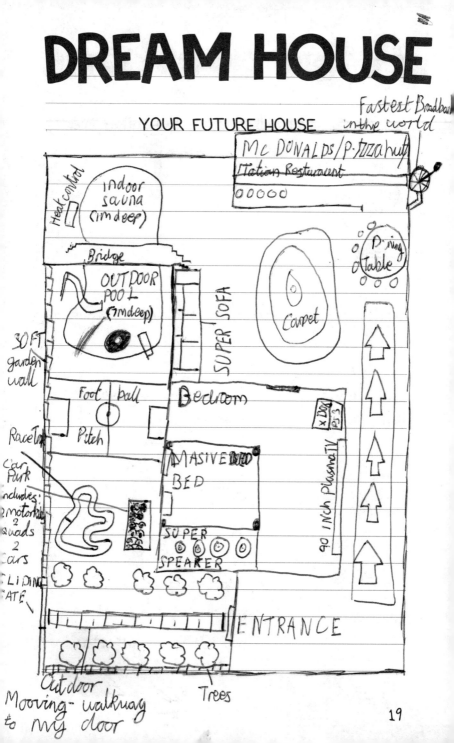

Fastest Broadband in the world

Mc DONALDS / P·Izza hut
Italian Resturaent
ooooo

Heat control

indoor sauna (1m deep)

Dining Table

Bridge

OUTDOOR POOL (7m deep)

Carpet

SUPER SOFA

30 FT garden wall

Foot ball Pitch

Bedroom

Race Track

Car Park includes: 2 motorbikes 2 quads 2 cars SLIDING GATE

x Box PS3

MASIVE BED

90 INCH Plasma TV

SUPER SPEAKER

ENTRANCE

Outdoor Mooving- walkway to my door

Trees

19

A few questions

What's the most embarrassing thing that ever
happened to someone who wasn't you?

HEYYY...

What's the worst thing you ever ate?

How many steps does it take you to jump into
bed after you turn off the light?

How much would you be willing to
pay for an extra hour of sleep
in the morning?

from GREG

Have you ever
pretended you were
sick so you could stay
home from school?

YOU POOR THING!

GROAN!

(NEW VIDEO GAME)

Does it get on your nerves when people skip?

TRA LA LA LA LA!

Did you ever do something bad that you never
got busted for?

Unfinished

Ugly Eugene

COMICS

Ugly Eugene

Make your

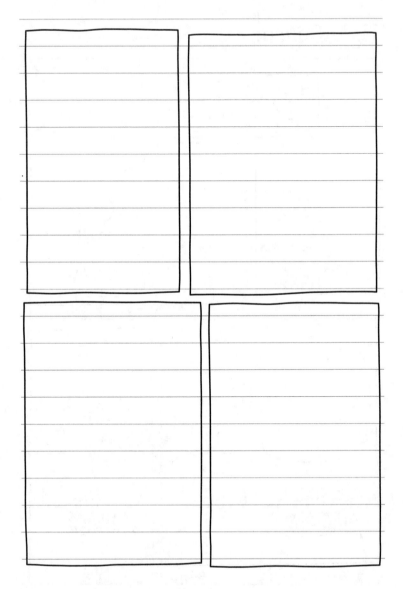

OWN comics

Good advice for

1. Don't use the bathroom on the second floor, because there aren't any stall doors in there.

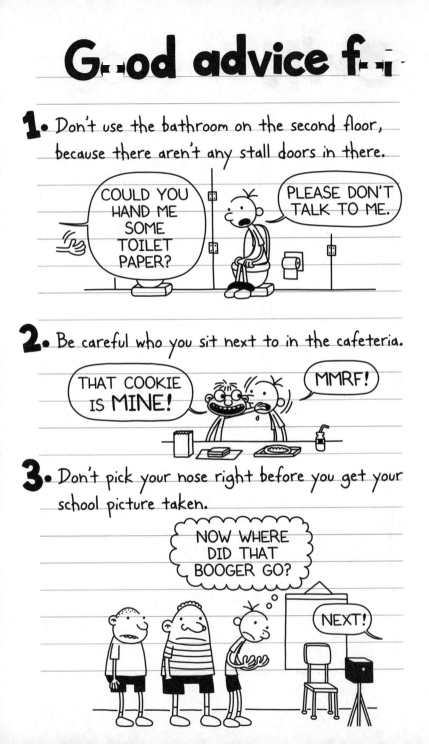

2. Be careful who you sit next to in the cafeteria.

3. Don't pick your nose right before you get your school picture taken.

next year's class

1.

2.

3.

4.

Draw your FAMILY

the way Greg Heffley would

Your FAVOURITES

TV show:

Band:

Sports team:

Food:

Celebrity:

Smell:

Villain:

Shoe brand:

Store:

Drink:

Cereal:

Super hero:

Candy:

Restaurant:

Athlete:

Game system:

Comic strip:

Magazine:

Car:

Your LEAST favourites

TV show:

Band:

Sports team:

Food:

Celebrity:

Smell:

Villain:

Shoe brand:

Store:

Drink:

Cereal:

Super hero:

Candy:

Restaurant:

Athlete:

Game system:

Comic strip:

Magazine:

Car:

Things you should do

☐ Stay up all night.

☐ Ride on a roller coaster with a loop in it.

☐ Get in a food fight. THWAP

☐ Get an autograph from a famous person.

☐ Get a hole-in-one in miniature golf.

☐ Give yourself a haircut.

☐ Write down an idea for an invention.

☐ Spend three nights in a row away from home.

☐ Mail someone a letter with a
real stamp and everything.

Dear
Gramma,
Please
send
money.

I ONLY HAVE
A FEW MORE
TO GO!

before you get old

☐ Go on a campout.

☐ Read a whole book with no pictures in it.

☐ Beat someone who's older than you in a footrace.

☐ Make it through a whole lollipop without biting it.

☐ Use a porta-potty.

OCCUPIED!

KNOCK KNOCK

☐ Score at least one point in an organized sport.

☐ Try out for a talent show.

EH?

Five things NOBODY KNOWS about you

BECAUSE THEY NEVER BOTHERED TO ASK

1.

2.

3.

4.

5.

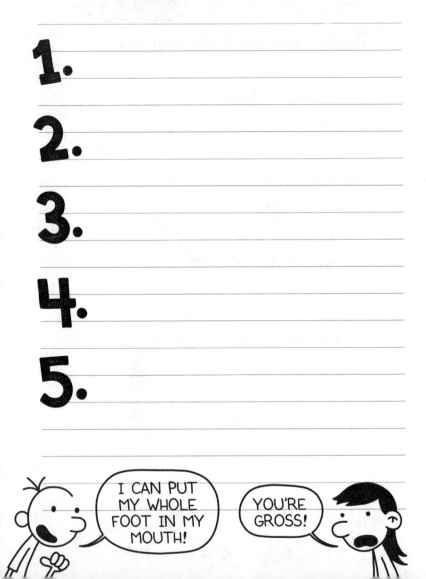

The WORST NIGHTMARE
you've ever had

Rules for your

1. Don't talk to me before 8:00 in the morning.

2. Don't make me sit next to my little brother on spaghetti night.

3. Don't walk into my room without knocking first.

4. Don't borrow my underwear under any circumstances.

FAMILY

1.

2.

3.

4.

Your life, by

Longest you've ever
gone without bathing:

_____

Most bowls of cereal you've
ever eaten at one time:

Longest you've ever been grounded: _____

Latest you've ever
been for school:

BLINK
BLINK

_____

Number of times you've
been chased by a dog:

SCREAM!

_____

Number of times you've been
locked out of the house:

_____

the numbers

Most hours you've spent
doing homework in one night:

_____

Most money you've ever saved up: _____

Length of the shortest book
you've ever used for a book report:

_____

Furthest distance you've ever walked:

_____

Longest you've ever gone without watching TV:

_____

Number of times   Number of times you've
you've been caught   got away with
picking your nose: picking your nose:

_____   _____

Unfinished

Li'l Cutie

" *Mommy, did my pencil go to heaven?* "

Li'l Cutie

" Go away, ya big eyed freak! "

COMICS

Li'l Cutie

Li'l Cutie

"_____"

Make your

"   "

OWN comics

[blank lined comic panel]

"   "

43

The FIRST FOUR LAWS you'll pass when you get elected president

1.

2.

3.

4.

" I hereby decree that no middle school student shalt have to take a shower after Phys Ed. "

The BADDEST THING
you ever did as a little kid

Practise your
SIGNATURE

You'll be famous one day, so let's face it...that signature of yours is gonna need some work. Use this page to practise your fancy new autograph.

List your INJURIES

SKINNED ELBOW
(TRIPPED ON KERB)

PLASTIC SHOE
STUCK UP NOSE

BUSTED CHIN (LEGS FELL
ASLEEP AFTER STAYING ON
THE TOILET TOO LONG)

BITE MARK ON
BACK OF LEG
(FREGLEY)

BROKEN PINKIE
(SLAMMED IN DOOR BY
LITTLE BROTHER)

A few questions

Do you believe in unicorns?

If you ever got to meet a unicorn, what would you ask it?

Have you ever drawn a picture that was so scary that it gave you nightmares?

SCREAM!

BOO

How many nights a week do you sleep in your parents' bed?

from ROWLEY

Have you ever tied your shoes without help from a grown-up?

GOOD BOY

Have you ever got sick from eating cherry lip gloss?

OH ROWLEY NOT AGAIN

GROAN

Are your friends jealous that you're a really good skipper?

TRA LA LA LA LA

CAN'T SKIP

The BIGGEST MISTAKES

1. Believing my older brother when he said it was "Pyjama Day" at my school.

2. Taking a dare that probably wasn't worth it.

3. Giving Timmy Brewer my empty soda bottle.

you've made so far

1.

2.

3.

Unfinished

Creighton the Cretin

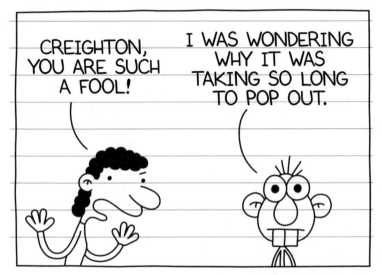

COMICS

Creighton the Cretin

Make your

OWN comics

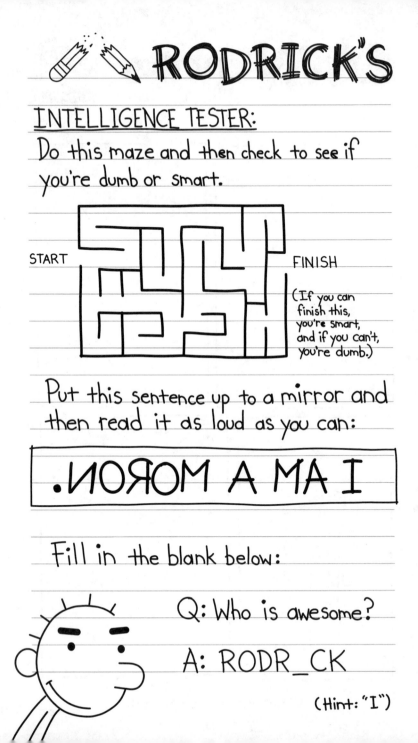

RODRICK'S

INTELLIGENCE TESTER:

Do this maze and then check to see if you're dumb or smart.

START   FINISH

(If you can finish this, you're smart, and if you can't, you're dumb.)

Put this sentence up to a mirror and then read it as loud as you can:

I AM A MORON.

Fill in the blank below:

Q: Who is awesome?

A: RODR_CK

(Hint: "I")

ACTIVITY PAGES

Answer this question yes or no <u>only</u>:

Q: Are you embarrassed that you pooped in your diaper today?

_____

Do you want to start a band? Well, I guess you're out of luck because the best name is already taken and that's Löded Diper. But if you still want to start a band then you can use this mix-and-match thing:*

FIRST HALF	SECOND HALF
Wikkid	Lizzerd
Nästy	Pigz
Vilent	Vömmit
Rabbid	Dagger
Killer	Syckle
Ransid	Smellz

* P.S. If you use one of these names, you owe me a hundred bucks.

# How well do you

Answer these questions, and then ask your friend the same things. Keep track of how many answers you got right.

FRIEND'S NAME: _____

Has your friend ever been
carsick?   _____

If your friend could meet any
celebrity, who would it be?   _____

Where was your friend born?   _____

Has your friend ever laughed
so hard that milk came out
of their nose?   _____

Has your friend ever been
sent to the principal's office? _____

9–10: YOU KNOW YOUR FRIEND SO WELL IT'S SCARY
6–8: NOT BAD...YOU KNOW YOUR FRIEND PRETTY WELL!

know your FRIEND?

What's your friend's favourite
junk food?   _____

Has your friend ever broken
a bone?   _____

When was the last time your
friend wet the bed?   _____

If your friend had to
permanently transform into
an animal, what animal would
it be?   _____

Is your friend secretly
afraid of clowns?   _____

Now count up your correct answers and look at the
scale below to see how you did.

2—5: DID YOU GUYS JUST MEET OR SOMETHING?
0—1: TIME TO GET A NEW FRIEND

If you had a

If you could go back in time and change the future, but you only had five minutes, where would you go?

If you could go back in time and witness any event in history, what would it be?

If you had to be stuck living in some time period in the past, what time period would you pick?

TIME MACHINE...

If you could go back and videotape one event from your own life, what would it be?

If you could go back and tell your past self one thing, what would it be?

If you could go forward in time and tell your future self something, what would it be?

YOU LOOK RIDICULOUS IN THOSE SOCKS!

FAH!

Totally awesome

The "Stand on One Foot" trick

STEP ONE: On your way home from school, bet your friend they can't stand on one foot for three minutes without talking.

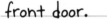

THAT'S SO CINCHY!

STEP TWO: While your friend stands on one foot, knock real hard on some crabby neighbour's front door.

KNOCK KNOCK KNOCK

?

STEP THREE: Run.

WHADDA YOU WANT?

ZIP

PRACTICAL JOKES

A JOKE YOU'VE PLAYED ON A FRIEND:

A JOKE YOU'VE PLAYED ON A FAMILY MEMBER:

A JOKE YOU'VE PLAYED ON A TEACHER:

Your DRESSING

If you end up being a famous musician or a movie star, you're gonna need to put together a list of things you'll need in your dressing room.

Requirements for Greg Heffley - page 1 of 9

3 litres of grape soda

2 extra-large pepperoni pizzas

2 dozen freshly baked chocolate-chip cookies

1 bowl of jelly beans (no pink or white ones)

1 popcorn machine

1 52-inch plasma TV

3 video-game consoles with 10 games apiece

1 soft-serve ice-cream machine

10 waffle cones

1 terry-cloth robe

1 pair of slippers

*** bathroom must have heated toilet seat

*** toilet paper must be name brand

ROOM requirements

You might as well get your list together now so that you're ready when you hit the big time.

Unfinished

The Amazing Fart Police

COMICS

The Amazing Fart Police

Make your

OWN comics

Your best ideas for

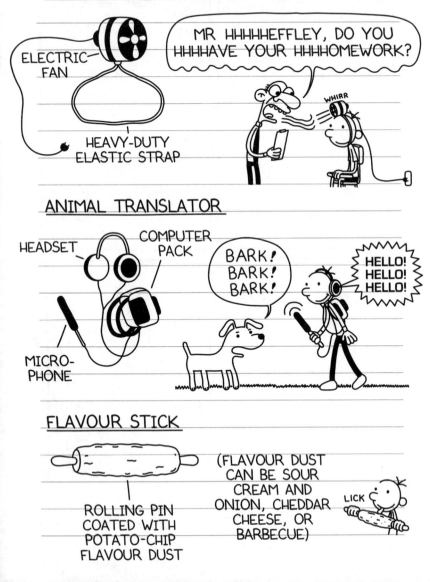

INVENTIONS

WRITE DOWN YOUR OWN AWESOME IDEAS
SO YOU CAN PROVE YOU CAME UP WITH
THEM BEFORE ANYONE ELSE.

Make a map of your

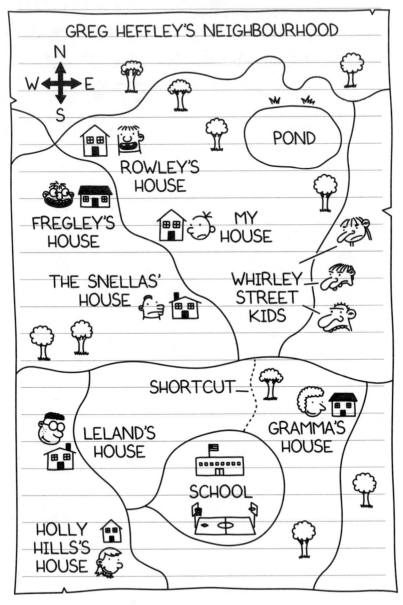

NEIGHBOURHOOD

YOUR NEIGHBOURHOOD

Make your own

GREETING CARDS

FRONT

INSIDE

FRONT

INSIDE

The BEST HOLIDAY
you ever went on

Make a LÖDED DIPER
CONCERT POSTER

Unfinished

Xtreme Sk8ers

COMICS

Xtreme Sk8ers

Make your

OWN comics

If you had

If you had the power to read other people's thoughts, would you really want to use it?

YES ☐ NO ☐

If you were a super hero, would you want to have a sidekick? YES ☐ NO ☐

SUPERPOWERS...

If you were a super hero, would you keep your identity secret?   YES ☐   NO ☐

Draw your FRIENDS

the way Greg Heffley would

A few questions

Do you ever put food in your belly button so you can have a snack later on?

Do animals ever use their thoughts to talk to you?

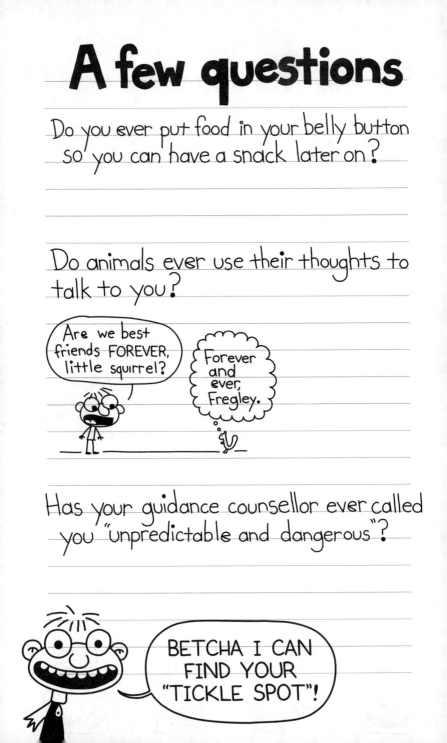

Has your guidance counsellor ever called you "unpredictable and dangerous"?

from FREGLEY

If you had a tail, what would you do with it?

Have you ever eaten a scab?

Do you wanna play "Diaper Whip"?

Have you ever been sent home from school early for "hygiene issues"?

You probably didn't wipe good enough again, Fregley.

Autographs

GET YOUR FRIENDS
TO WRITE STUFF
IN THIS BOOK.

Autographs

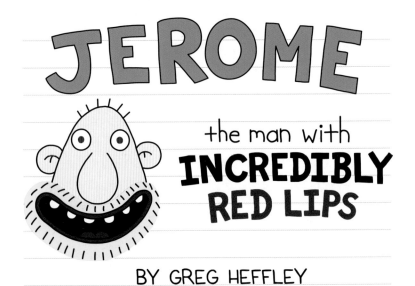

JEROME

the man with
INCREDIBLY
RED LIPS

BY GREG HEFFLEY

NEXT WEEK: THE FART POLICE INVADE A BURRITO FACTORY

Create your own COVER

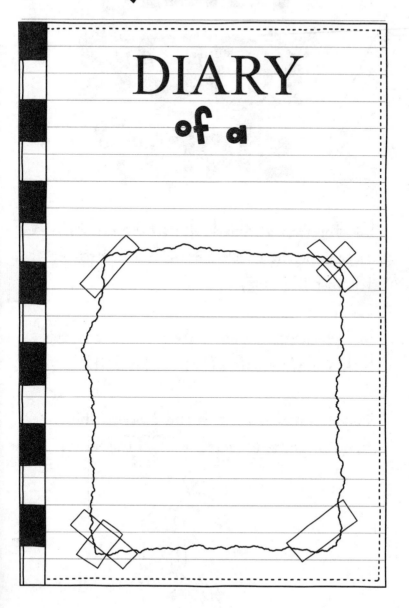

DIARY

of a

What's YOUR story?

Use the rest of this book to keep a daily journal, write a novel, draw comic strips, or tell your life story.

But whatever you do, make sure you put this book someplace safe after you finish it.

Because when you're rich and famous, this thing is gonna be worth a FORTUNE.

ABOUT THE AUTHOR

(THAT'S YOU)

ACKNOWLEDGEMENTS

(THE PEOPLE YOU WANT TO THANK)

Now see how the expert does it in this EXCLUSIVE extract from

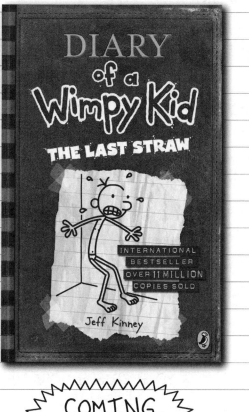

JANUARY

<u>New Year's Day</u>

You know how you're supposed to come up with a list of "resolutions" at the beginning of the year to try to make yourself a better person?

Well, the problem is it's not easy for me to think of ways to improve myself, because I'm already pretty much one of the best people I know.

So this year my resolution is to try to help OTHER people improve. But the thing I'm finding out is that some people don't really appreciate it when you're trying to be helpful.

One thing I noticed right off the bat is that the people in my family are doing a lousy job sticking to THEIR New Year's resolutions.

Mom said she was gonna start going to the gym today, but she spent the whole afternoon watching TV.

And Dad said he was gonna go on a strict diet, but after dinner I caught him out in the garage, stuffing his face with brownies.

SLORK
SLORK

Even my little brother, Manny, couldn't stick with his resolution.

This morning he told everyone that he's a "big boy" and he's giving up his pacifier for good. Then he threw his favourite binkie in the trash.

Well, THAT New Year's resolution didn't even last a full MINUTE.

The only person in my family who didn't come up with a resolution is my older brother, Rodrick, and that's a pity because his list should be about a mile and a half long.

So I decided to come up with a programme to help Rodrick be a better person. I called my plan "Three Strikes and You're Out". The basic idea was that every time I saw Rodrick messing up, I'd mark a little "X" on his chart.

Well, Rodrick got all three strikes before I even had a chance to decide what "You're Out" meant.

PUNCH
PUNCH
PUNCH

Anyway, I'm starting to wonder if I should just bag MY resolution, too. It's a lot of work, and so far I haven't really made any progress.

Besides, after I reminded Mom for like the billionth time to stop chewing her crisps so loud, she made a really good point. She said, "Everyone can't be as perfect as YOU, Gregory." And from what I've seen so far I think she's right.

Thursday

Dad is giving this diet thing another try, and that's bad news for me. He's gone about three days without eating any chocolate, and he's been SUPER cranky.

The other day, after Dad woke me up and told me to get ready for school, I accidentally fell back asleep. Believe me, that's the last time I'll make THAT mistake.

Part of the problem is that Dad always wakes me up before Mom's out of the shower, so I know that I still have like ten more minutes before I need to get out of bed for real.

Yesterday I came up with a pretty good way to get some extra sleep time without making Dad mad. After he woke me up, I took all of my blankets down the hall with me and waited outside the bathroom for my turn in the shower.

Then I lay down right on top of the heater vent. And when the furnace was blowing, the experience was even BETTER than being in bed.

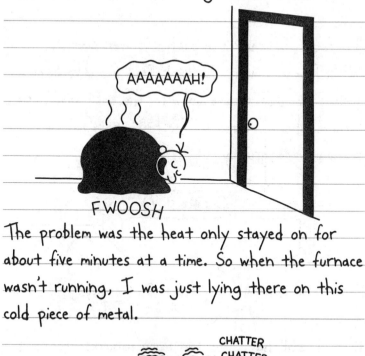

The problem was the heat only stayed on for about five minutes at a time. So when the furnace wasn't running, I was just lying there on this cold piece of metal.

This morning, while I was waiting for Mom to be done with her shower, I remembered someone gave her a bathrobe for Christmas. So I went into her closet and got it.

Let me just say that was one of the smartest moves I've ever made. Wearing that thing was like being wrapped in a big, fluffy towel that just came out of the dryer.

In fact, I liked it so much, I even wore it AFTER my shower. I think Dad might've been jealous HE didn't come up with the robe idea first, because when I came to the kitchen table, he seemed extra grumpy.

MORNIN'!

I tell you, women have the right idea with this bathrobe thing. Now I'm wondering what ELSE I'm missing out on.

I just wish I had asked for my own bathrobe for Christmas, because I'm sure Mom is gonna make me give hers back.

I struck out on gifts again this year. I knew I was in for a rough day when I came downstairs on Christmas morning and the only presents in my stocking were a stick of deodorant and a "travel dictionary".

I guess once you're in middle school, grown-ups decide you're too old for toys or anything that's actually fun.

But then they still expect you to be all excited when you open the lame gifts they get you.

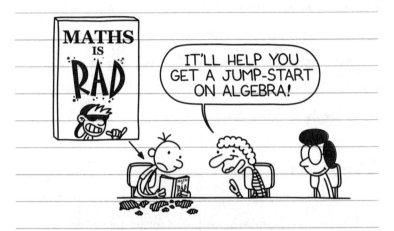

Most of my gifts this year were books or clothes. The closest thing I got to a toy was a present from Uncle Charlie.

When I unwrapped Uncle Charlie's gift, I didn't even know what it was supposed to be. It was this big plastic ring with a net attached to it.

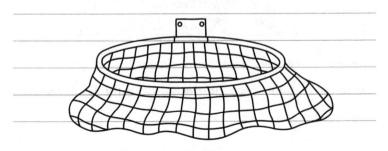

Uncle Charlie explained that it was a "Laundry Hoop" for my bedroom. He said I was supposed to hang the Laundry Hoop on the back of my door and it would make putting away my dirty clothes "fun".

At first I thought it was a joke, but then I realized Uncle Charlie was serious. So I had to explain to him that I don't actually DO my own laundry.

I told him I just throw my dirty clothes on the floor, and Mom picks them up and takes them downstairs to the laundry room.

Then, a few days later, everything comes back to me in nice, folded piles.

I told Uncle Charlie he should just return the Laundry Hoop and give me cash so I could buy something I'd actually USE.

That's when Mom spoke up. She told Uncle Charlie she thought the Laundry Hoop was a GREAT idea.

Then she said that from now on I'd be doing my OWN laundry. So, basically, it ends up that Uncle Charlie got me a chore for Christmas.

It really stinks that I got such crummy gifts this year. I put in a lot of effort buttering people up for the past few months, and I thought it would pay off on Christmas.

Now that I'm responsible for my own laundry, I guess I'm kind of GLAD I got a bunch of clothes. I might actually make it through the whole school year before I run out of clean stuff to wear.

It all started with a Scarecrow

Puffin is well over sixty years old.
Sounds ancient, doesn't it? But Puffin has never been
so lively. We're always on the lookout for the next big
idea, which is how it began all those years ago.

Penguin Books was a big idea from the mind of
a man called Allen Lane, who in 1935 invented
the quality paperback and changed the world.
**And from great Penguins, great Puffins grew,
changing the face of children's books forever.**

The first four Puffin Picture Books were hatched in 1940 and the
first Puffin story book featured a man with broomstick arms called
Worzel Gummidge. In 1967 Kaye Webb, Puffin Editor, started the
Puffin Club, promising to **'make children into readers'.**
She kept that promise and over 200,000 children became
devoted Puffineers through their quarterly installments of
Puffin Post, which is now back for a new generation.

Many years from now, we hope you'll look back and
remember Puffin with a smile. **No matter what your age
or what you're into, there's a Puffin for everyone.**
The possibilities are endless, but one thing is for sure:
whether it's a picture book or a paperback, a sticker book
or a hardback, **if it's got that little Puffin
on it – it's bound to be good.**